Ace Ghosts

The Ghosts of CREAKIE HALL in Ace Ghosts

Karen Wallace
and Tony Ross

Catnip

CATNIP BOOKS
Published by Catnip Publishing Ltd
Quality Court off Chancery Lane
London WC2A 1HR

This edition first published 2010

First published by Hamish Hamilton Ltd 1996
3 5 7 9 10 8 6 4 2

A CIP catalogue record for this book is available from the
British Library.

ISBN 978 1 846470 92 9

Printed in Poland

www.catnippublishing.co.uk

To Tim 'n' Belinda

Chapter 1

Miasma Bogey-Mandeville put down her cards and stared out of the attic window of Creakie Hall. The sky was a ghostly silver just like Miasma's long bony face and the sun was as orange as her knee-length hair.

Miasma loved the view from her attic. It hadn't changed for hundreds of years. And nor for that matter had she.

Miasma closed her cat-green eyes and smiled. She liked things to stay the same. Creakie Hall was still crumbling. The murky lake still bubbled with thousands of bullfrogs. And best of all, the maze with its high thick hedges had been kept just as it always was. Miasma chuckled. Once you were lost, it was like a prison.

A huge black bird circled above the maze. It had a long skinny neck and a horrible hooked beak.

It looked liked a vulture. But it wasn't. Miasma pursed her lips. It was Marmaduke, her husband, up to his usual tricks.

She picked up her cards and looked at them. Then she sneaked a quick look at Marmaduke's on the other side of the table. She was winning.

It wasn't a bad life on the top floor of Creakie Hall, thought Miasma. Nobody knew she and Marmaduke were there so nobody bothered them. And for the most part they

didn't bother anyone either. They certainly didn't run up and down stairs carrying their heads in their hands or rattling ghostly chains.

Miasma looked out of the window again. It was true that *sometimes* Marmaduke did get restless . . .

On the lawn below, Osbert Codseye was cutting the grass. Miasma watched Marmaduke's vulture shadow pass over him. She watched Osbert's mouth drop open and the lawn mower drive straight across the grass, through a flowerbed and into the lake.

'Marmaduke!' cried Miasma. 'Come back! How many times do I have to tell you? Flesh'n'bloods don't like vultures.'

A cold breeze fluttered through the room and Marmaduke Bogey-Mandeville appeared in front of her. He was tall with black curling hair and wore an old-fashioned ruff at his neck. A long sword clanked at his belt.

'What's wrong with vultures?' he asked in a sulky voice.

Miasma rolled her eyes. 'Nothing as far as *we're* concerned,' she said.

'But flesh'n'bloods prefer friendly birds like sparrows or robins.' She shrugged and ran her hands through her head. 'Something about their table manners.'

Marmaduke scowled. 'Well, I don't like friendly birds like sparrows or robins,' he said. 'They're *boring*.' He knocked his cards onto the floor. 'And I'm fed up playing poker.'

Miasma's green eyes opened wide.

'But spookypet!' she cried. 'We've been playing poker since 1665!' She looked at the four aces in her hand. 'And I'm just getting good at it.'

'That's another thing I'm fed up with,' muttered Marmaduke. 'And don't call me spookypet.'

Suddenly, a huge ghostly silver cat jumped through the door into the room. His name was Cromwell and he had lived in Creakie Hall since he was a kitten, round about the time of the first poker game in 1665.

Cromwell's turquoise eyes bulged. His tail whirled round and he somersaulted from chair to chair.

Finally he landed upside down on the card table between them, yowling hideously.

Marmaduke spoke first. 'I think Cromwell's trying to tell us something,' he said in a low voice.

A shiver went straight through Miasma's stomach and cracked a mirror on the opposite wall. It was the moment she had been dreading for over three hundred years.

'Something's *changing* at Creakie Hall,' she said slowly. 'I can feel it in my bones. What are we going to do?'

'Storm the ramparts!' shouted Marmaduke, pulling out his sword. 'Fire the cannons! Boil the –'

'Rubbish!' cried Miasma. Her green eyes narrowed. 'We have to be sneaky about this. First, we have to find out *exactly* what's going on.'

Marmaduke turned back into a vulture and jumped onto the window-sill. He cocked his head to one side.

'Leave it to me,' he croaked horribly.

Miasma glared at him. 'You're not going anywhere looking like *that*!' she said.

She stood up and laid her cards face up on the table. Marmaduke pretended not to see them.

'*I'll* go,' she said in a firm voice. 'We don't want to scare them this time.'

And without another word she turned herself into a huge crocodile and slithered through the wall.

Aunt Gardenia Bogey-Mandeville sat on one side of a long table in the dining room of Creakie Hall. Her niece and nephew, Polly and George, sat beside her.

They hadn't noticed a huge crocodile standing on its hind legs peering in at the window.

In front of Aunt Gardenia, the

dining room table was covered in letters. They were letters from builders and plumbers and electricians and they all said the same thing. Creakie Hall was falling down.

Aunt Gardenia picked up one letter in particular. It was signed with a big backward sloping scrawl. '*Dear Miss Gardenia,*' she read in her sweet clear voice.

'*So what if Creakie Hall has been in your family for hundreds of years. Big deal. Take a tip from me. Sell it quick. Buy a bungalow.*

Your friendly bank manager,

Ed Stinge.

P.S. And I ain't lending you no money.'

Aunt Gardenia peered over the top of her little gold glasses.

'So that's why I asked you here today,' she said to Polly and George. 'That naughty Mr Stinge has turned down my request for a loan. If we can't think of a way of making money, Creakie Hall will have to be sold.'

'But what are we going to do?' asked Polly.

'There's a crocodile at the window!' shouted George.

'Don't be silly, darling,' said Aunt Gardenia. 'This is serious.' She picked up her knitting from an enormous bag at her feet. *Clack, clack, clack,* went the needles.

'As you know, my best ideas come when I knit,' said Aunt Gardenia with her little smile.

Polly and George nodded politely. Almost everything at Creakie Hall had a cosy knitted cover.

Even the lawn mower.

'So!' cried Aunt Gardenia, her eyes shining. 'What do you think of this?' She held her hands wide apart.

Between them was a banner knitted in deep purple wool. CREAKIE HALL HOTEL – OPEN TO EVERYONE was knitted in shiny gold letters across the front.

At that moment, Osbert Codseye staggered into the room. He was covered in mud and his eyes rolled in his head.

'Gracious!' cried Aunt Gardenia, putting down her banner. 'Osbert! You look as if you've seen a ghost!'

Osbert Codseye opened his mouth to speak. He wanted to tell them about the vulture in the garden. How he had seen it disappear through the attic window. He wanted to tell them that something peculiar was going on. Then he saw a huge crocodile staring at him from the window. Osbert Codseye crumpled to the floor in a dead faint.

CHAPTER 2

POLLY AND GEORGE climbed the wide, winding stairs to their playroom. As they passed the front window, they could see Aunt Gardenia and Osbert Codseye tying the knitted purple banner to the main gates of Creakie Hall.

'It's all very well turning Creakie Hall into a hotel,' said Polly. 'But who's going to run it?'

'And who's going to sleep in the lumpy beds with the knitted sheets?' said George.

Polly giggled. 'Or put up with the

bullfrogs at night,' she said. 'There must be thousands of them by now.'

'If only I could train them,' cried George. He spun around. 'I can see it now! Creakie Hall Hotel presents the Bogey-Mandeville Bullfrog Band!'

'People would come from miles away!' shouted Polly, jumping up and down. 'All our troubles would be —' She froze and pointed to the end of the dark wooden hall. 'What's *that*?'

A huge cat was sitting on the carpet. It was the strangest-looking cat they had ever seen. Its fur was a ghostly silver and its eyes were turquoise. As soon as the cat saw Polly and George both staring, it got up and walked purposefully down the corridor.

'George,' whispered Polly. 'I think this cat wants us to follow it.'

George looked puzzled.

'But there's nowhere to go up there,'
he said. 'The corridor's a dead end.'

Ahead of them the cat was walking
solemnly down the corridor.

'Let's follow him anyway,' whispered
Polly.

Suddenly a door they had never seen before appeared in the wall in front of them. It was a heavy, old-fashioned door with a big iron lock.

George was just about to put out his hand to see if it was real, when the cat walked straight through it.

A second later the door swung open.

Polly and George found themselves staring face to face with two people

who were somehow strangely familiar. And although it is rude to stare, Polly and George stared until they thought their eyes would fall out.

Then Polly remembered where she had seen them before.

'Are you the, um, people whose portraits are in the front hall?' she stammered, thinking at the same time she had gone completely mad.

Marmaduke   Bogey-Mandeville squared his shoulders and grabbed the hilt of his sword just like in his portrait.

'That's me,' he cried.

Miasma Bogey-Mandeville stepped up beside him and crossed her hands demurely in front of her long dress.

'And this is me,' she said with a wolfish grin.

Now it was George's turn to wonder if he had gone mad. There was something about that grin. He had seen it before. But when he remembered where, that seemed even crazier than what was happening now.

'Were you the crocodile at the window?' he asked, at last.

Miasma crowed with delight. 'I certainly was,' she cried. 'I heard every word.'

'That's why we, um, *invited* you here,' said Marmaduke, looking serious. 'We want to help.'

'Help?' said Polly in a puzzled voice.

'Help save Creakie Hall,' Miasma said, helpfully.

'And to tell you the truth, we

were both getting rather bored up here,' explained Marmaduke. 'We've been playing cards since 1665 and –'

'*I'm* not bored,' interrupted Miasma. She fiddled with the locket at her neck. 'Well, maybe just a little bit.'

George decided the direct approach was the best one.

'What can you do?' he asked.

'Anything!' cried Miasma and Marmaduke.

'And anything we can't do, we'll learn,' said Miasma.

Polly and George looked at each other. The whole thing was totally and completely unbelievable. First there was the bank manager refusing to lend Creakie Hall any money. Then there was Aunt Gardenia deciding to turn it into a hotel to raise their own money. Now there were two goofy ghosts offering to

do *anything* to help. Which was all very well, but –

'The point is,' said Polly, carefully, 'that some things have changed since your day.' She paused. 'In fact almost everything has –'

'It certainly has,' interrupted Miasma. 'And I quite agree with you. The old ways were the best ways.' She turned to look at Marmaduke.

'Absolutely, ghostykins,' he said, smiling fondly at her.

Polly looked helplessly at George.

George took a big breath. 'Of course, we'd have to get a few things straight first,' he said in his deepest voice.

'Of course,' said Marmaduke and Miasma.

'Definitely no appearing and disappearing,' said George.

'Definitely not,' said Marmaduke and Miasma.

'And *strictly* no crocodiles,' said Polly.

'How about vultures?' asked Marmaduke.

'No vultures,' said Polly, firmly.

'Excellent,' cried Miasma. 'We agree! We'll start immediately!'

And before George and Polly had time to reply, Miasma and Marmaduke disappeared.

'Ooops,' said Miasma's voice from somewhere near the ceiling. 'We weren't supposed to do that.'

'You did it first.'

'Didn't.'

'Did.'

'*Didn't.*'

Then both voices faded away.

Polly looked at George.

'Is this real?' she said.

George nodded. 'I think so.' He paused. 'Your eyes are the same colour as hers.'

'And you've got black hair like he has,' said Polly, slowly.

'I think we should introduce them to Aunt Gardenia,' said George.

'Polly! George!' It was Aunt Gardenia's voice coming from the bottom of the stairs. She sounded breathless and excited.

'I think they've already met,' said Polly.

CHAPTER 3

AUNT GARDENIA WAS standing in the front hall beside Marmaduke and Miasma. Only now Marmaduke and Miasma looked completely different. Miasma's knee-length hair was piled on top of her head and she was wearing a black-and-white maid's uniform. Marmaduke was dressed entirely in white with a big chef's hat. A meat cleaver dangled at his waist.

Behind them stood Osbert Codseye clutching the dining-room door and grinning weakly.

'What clever children you are!' cried Aunt Gardenia. 'Just when Osbert and I were asking ourselves who would help run the hotel, you found these two lovely people.' She beamed at Polly and George. 'Where *on earth* did you meet?'

'Um,' said Polly.

'Er,' said George.

'We were just hanging around!' cried Miasma with her wolfish grin.

Aunt Gardenia laughed. 'Osbert and I are delighted,' she said. 'Especially since we have our first booking.' Aunt Gardenia beamed. 'They sound terribly nice. They were driving past the front gates and saw my knitted banner.'

'And *everything* will be ready in time,' promised Miasma with a gleam in her cat-shaped eyes. As she spoke, a bucket and mop appeared from the cupboard and a feather duster tucked itself under her arm.

Polly's face went white.

'Oops,' said Miasma, putting her hand over her mouth.

'Gracious,' said Aunt Gardenia. 'Modern machines are so *clever* these days.'

'They certainly are,' agreed Miasma.

And she set off upstairs with the bucket, the broom, the feather duster and two Hoovers following after her.

There was a soft *thud* behind them. Osbert Codseye had slumped to the floor.

'Dear, oh dear,' murmured Aunt Gardenia, picking up her enormous knitting bag. 'I do believe a cosy cover will make Osbert feel better.'

Above them the ceiling shook with bangs and crashes.

'And I must find Miasma,' cried Polly, racing upstairs.

'And I'll help Marmaduke in the kitchen,' said George, nervously.

'Excellent,' cried Marmaduke, patting his meat cleaver. 'Come and see what I've done *already*!'

Upstairs all the bedrooms looked the same. The furniture was floating near the ceiling, the cobwebs had been sprayed with gold paint, the curtains were on the beds and all the pictures were upside down. There was no sign of Miasma.

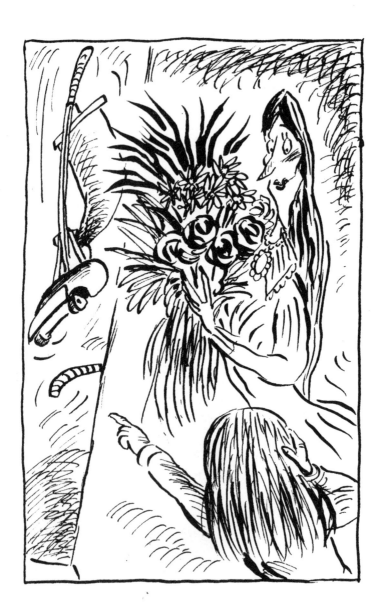

Polly ran down the corridor, past a bucket and mop that appeared to be arguing and dodged two Hoovers that were racing each other up and down the wall.

'Almost ready!' cried Miasma, appearing from round a corner with a huge armful of flowers. 'Just a little something in each room. It's the details that count, don't you think?'

'Miasma,' said Polly. 'About the furniture in the bedrooms —'

'Oh, don't worry about *that*!' cried Miasma. 'I left the Hoovers and the bucket and mop in charge.'

Polly took a deep breath. This was going to be even more difficult than she had imagined.

'Miasma,' she said, holding her head in her hands, 'the bucket and mop are arguing and the hoovers are racing each other along the wall.'

Miasma's green eyes flashed.

'How dare they?' she cried. 'Just wait till I get my hands on them!' With that she dumped the flowers on the floor and strode furiously down the corridor.

Polly bent to pick up the flowers. Behind her there was a terrible clanking and the hiss of flying sparks.

'And there won't be a next time,' yelled Miasma from inside one of the bedrooms. 'You'll be twigs and rushes and that'll be *that*!'

Then to Polly's amazement, she heard the even sound of a Hoover moving back and forth across a carpet and the slop and squeeze of a wet mop cleaning a wooden floor.

'That's better,' said Miasma, sternly.

A minute later, her head appeared out of a bedroom with something draped over her arm.

'What's *this*?' she asked Polly. 'It looks really *peculiar*.'

It was one of Aunt Gardenia's knitted sheets and for the first time in her life, Polly thought it was the most normal thing she had ever seen.

'Polly!' shouted George from the front hall.

There was a crunch of gravel.

'The guests are here!'

CHAPTER 4

POLLY SLID HALFWAY downstairs and crouched behind the banisters just in time to see two people get out of a big black car. One of them was wearing a pinstripe suit that was too tight. He had a blotchy fussy-looking red face and piggy black eyes.

'That's Rupert Cudgel,' said George creeping up beside her. 'I looked in the register book. The other one's Amelia Whinge.'

Amelia Whinge wore a beige dress that hung on her bony shoulders like a raincoat on a scarecrow. She had

a long thin nose and a mouth that
was a hard slash across her face.

The two of them stared at Creakie
Hall as if they could see every loose
nail and crumbling corner.

'Where's Aunt Gardenia?' whispered
Polly.

'She's in the garden comforting Osbert Codseye,' said George. 'Something terrible has happened. All his flowers —'

'Oh, no,' moaned Polly, as she remembered Miasma's huge armful. 'How's Marmaduke?'

'Terrific,' said George. He rolled his eyes. 'Every time he chops his hand off another one appears. The table is covered in stuffed swans and roast boars and there's a huge cauldron of boiling oil —'

'*Boiling oil?*'

George shrugged. 'Something about defending the ramparts,' he muttered.

'Look!' said Polly, pointing to the front hall.

Below them Rupert Cudgel was opening doors, stepping into rooms, sniffing, and stepping out again. Amelia Whinge crept about looking behind pictures and lifting up ornaments.

'Do you think they're burglars?' whispered George.

'I don't know,' said Polly, 'but we can't stay here.'

She stood up and walked down the stairs.

'Welcome to Creakie Hall Hotel,' she said in her friendliest voice.

'A rather poor welcome, I'd say,' whined Amelia Whinge.

'Terrible service,' said Rupert Cudgel. 'Where are our rooms?'

'I'm afraid they're not quite ready,' said Polly, smiling sweetly. 'Perhaps you'd like —'

The sitting room door mysteriously opened. There was a roaring fire and the sound of a harp playing.

'Cocktails?' cried Miasma.

Polly spun round. Miasma was

wearing a shocking pink body stocking with thigh-length silver boots. Her long orange hair frizzed out on either side of a white lacy cap.

'They're my own recipe,' said Miasma, striding behind the bar. She threw back her head and laughed like a fire bell. 'They're guaranteed to restore spirits.'

Rupert and Amelia sipped at the glasses of misty green liquid.

'What's in them?' hissed Polly.

'Warm pond water and minced frog spawn,' replied Miasma in a loud whisper.

'I think I need some air,' said Amelia Whinge in a strangled voice.

'What did she say?' asked Rupert Cudgel, suspiciously.

'Fresh lime juice and crushed kiwi fruit,' said Polly quickly. 'It's a house speciality.'

'Cocktails! How charming!' said
Aunt Gardenia at the door. Beside
her stood Osbert Codseye in
something that looked like a knitted
diving suit.

'My great-grandmother used to
make a cocktail like this,' continued
Aunt Gardenia, sipping at her glass.
'Except she put frog –'

'Frog spawn and bullfrogs are two of my favourite things!' shouted George, desperately.

'Mine, too!' cried Miasma in a delighted voice.

Rupert Cudgel looked around the room.

'Where is Amelia Whinge?' he muttered.

'She went to get some fresh air,' said Aunt Gardenia. 'Marmaduke said he would look after her.'

A weak cry floated in through the open window. Everyone looked out. A huge bird with a horrible hooked beak was circling round and round the maze. The weak cry grew more desperate.

'Marmaduke!' shouted Miasma. 'What did I tell you about vultures?'

Polly put her hands over her eyes.

Osbert Codseye slumped to the floor.

'Gracious me!' murmured Aunt Gardenia. 'Look at the time. I must dress for dinner.' She propped Osbert Codseye against the wall and shook hands with Rupert Cudgel. 'I do hope you enjoy your stay with us,' she said, smiling sweetly.

Rupert Cudgel tried to speak but no words came.

'You mustn't be shy, dear,' said Aunt Gardenia, patting his arm. 'Creakie Hall Hotel is home from home, you know.'

A wave of gravel sprayed the window and a beaten-up truck screeched to a halt outside the front door. Far away beyond the main drive, there was a sound of police sirens. Then it faded into the air and disappeared.

A tubby little man with a bald head jumped out of the truck and

walked neatly up the front steps and
into the front hall. He was dressed in
a pair of blue overalls with black
arrows all over them.

He grabbed Aunt Gardenia's
hand and pumped it up and down.
'Pleased to meet ya,' cried the little
man. 'The name's Loot, Barney Loot.'

He flashed a set of shiny white teeth. 'Thing is, we're making this, um, prison escape movie. It's all about this, um, nice guy who breaks outta jail, gives the police the slip and goes into the world to start a new life.' He laughed and his blue eyes twinkled. 'It's my favourite story.'

'It sounds wonderful,' cried Aunt Gardenia. 'I love a movie with a happy ending.'

'So do I!' cried Barney Loot. 'So when I saw your banner, I said to myself, Barney, this is just the place to hold out for a while.'

'And we hold out a warm welcome to you, too, Mr Loot,' replied Aunt Gardenia, sweetly. 'Have a cocktail.'

'First things first,' said Barney Loot holding up a stubby finger. 'D'ya mind if I pay ya later?'

'Not at all, dear,' said Aunt

Gardenia. 'Osbert and I would be delighted, wouldn't we Osbert?'

Osbert Codseye moaned inside his knitted suit.

'Osbert's having a bad day,' whispered Aunt Gardenia. 'Why only this afternoon –'

Amelia Whinge staggered into the room. Her face was grey and her thin mouth had virtually disappeared.

'Amelia!' cried Rupert Cudgel, mopping his brow with a spotted handkerchief. 'What's wrong?'

Amelia Whinge stared at him with wild eyes. 'That maze,' she gasped. 'It's –'

'Just like a prison,' chuckled Miasma.

Rupert Cudgel glared at her.

'Where are our rooms?' he asked in an icy voice.

'Yummy cocktails!' cried Barney Loot, pouring a second one down his throat. 'Funny though, tastes just like –'

'I'll take you to your rooms,' said Polly, steering Rupert and Amelia towards the stairs. 'I think they're ready now.'

And they were.

There was a fire in each one, even though there was no fireplace.

Miasma had tried very hard with the bathrooms, too. The bath was full of steaming pond water and floating lily pads. A large bullfrog was waiting on each one to welcome them.

CHAPTER 5

'CLOSE YOUR EYES! It's a surprise!' cried Marmaduke, outside the dining room.

Polly and George squeezed their eyes shut and hoped for the best. After the bedrooms, they didn't want any more surprises for a very long time.

The dining room door squeaked as it was pulled open.

'Whaddyathink of this?' cried Marmaduke, who had been listening to pop radio all afternoon. 'Ain't it the greatest?'

Polly gasped. George made a strange gurgling noise in the back of his throat.

The room was decorated with stuffed animal heads and long gleaming bones. In the middle, Miasma turned a huge pig on a spit and shooed away the mangy dogs that snuffled for titbits in the dirty straw on the floor.

'It's a medieval banquet!' cried Marmaduke. 'Don'tcha just love it?'

'It's a triumph, dear,' agreed, Aunt Gardenia, gliding into the room in a long dress with lots of rosebuds and ruffles.

Beside her, Osbert Codseye wore a black dinner jacket and bow tie over his knitted suit.

'Where's *our* table?' demanded Rupert Cudgel from the door. He had a mean look on his face. Rupert

Cudgel hated bullfrogs and Amelia Whinge was allergic to lily pads.

There was only one long table in the room.

'Don't worry,' said Aunt Gardenia sweetly. 'We all eat together at Creakie Hall.'

Rupert Cudgel and Amelia Whinge sat down at the end of the table as far away as possible from everybody else.

'I need a drink,' whined Amelia.

'Half a bottle of red and half a bottle of white wine,' ordered Rupert in a rude voice. 'And chop, chop,' he added, snapping his fingers twice at Marmaduke. 'We're in a hurry.'

Two wine bottles appeared in Marmaduke's hands.

'Are you a waiter or a wizard?' sneered Rupert Cudgel. 'I said, half bottles.'

Marmaduke looked puzzled for a moment, then he picked up his cleaver.

'Oh, no,' muttered George.

Chop! Chop! Marmaduke handed Rupert two half bottles of wine.

'Pig!' cried Miasma, holding out a plateful of food towards Rupert Cudgel.

'I beg your pardon,' cried Rupert.

'Would you like some roast boar,'
said Polly, jumping up from her chair.

'Bird brain!' shouted Marmaduke
in Amelia Whinge's ear.

'What?' yelled Amelia.

'Or a delicious piece of stuffed
swan?' said George.

'Just bread,' muttered Rupert.

'And a carrot,' whined Amelia.

'Whattaguy!' cried Marmaduke,
dropping a thick wedge of bread in
front of Rupert's twitching purple

face. It was piled high with pigs' ears, swans' beaks and one crispy curly tail.

'And for the lady!'

The carrot had three roast sparrows perched on it. Amelia Whinge took one look and fell face first into her soup bowl.

'Water!' shouted Rupert Cudgel. Then he seemed to remember something and changed his mind. 'No! Not water!' he screamed.

Just in time, Amelia Whinge staggered to her feet and watched hollow-eyed as Marmaduke poured a whole jug of pond water into her soup bowl.

'Marmaduke!' cried Miasma, rushing across the room and forcing Amelia back into her chair. 'You'll ruin her appetite!'

At the other end of the table Barney Loot sat with a large snowy napkin around his neck, munching through his third plate of meaty bones.

'Every one a winner!' cried Barney Loot each time he threw a bone to the dogs snapping and snarling on the other side of the room.

In the middle of the table Aunt Gardenia smiled sweetly. Even Osbert Codseye had cheered up. His second cocktail had two extra dollops of frog spawn in it.

Miasma caught Marmaduke's eye and winked. Everything seemed to be going splendidly. What's more, it was such *fun*, helping out after all those years in the attic.

Now it was time for their big surprise. Polly and George would just *love* it. Miasma grinned to herself.

Hadn't she heard them planning exactly the same thing in the corridor outside their attic?

Marmaduke winked back and climbed onto the table. He didn't look like a chef any more. He was dressed in a tail coat and he had a conductor's baton in his hands.

Polly hid behind her hands.

George held his breath.

Marmaduke whacked his baton against his shoe. Five hundred bull-frogs, a few carrying instruments, jumped through the window. They took their places and began to sing.

It was the Bogey-Mandeville Bullfrog Band!

Polly's eyes popped out of her head.

'George!' she whispered. 'Do you remember –?'

'Of course I do,' said George, hugging himself with delight.

Barney Loot turned to Aunt Gardenia.

'May I ask you a favour, ma'am?' he whispered.

'Certainly, Mr Loot,' replied Aunt Gardenia, happily.

'The thing is,' began Barney Loot, 'this movie I'm making. Well,

it's not just above *one* nice guy who breaks outta jail and goes into the world to start a new life. It's about *fifty* nice guys.'

'How lovely!' cried Aunt Gardenia, clapping her hands. 'So your movie really *does* have a happy ending.'

Barney Loot swallowed. 'That's

what I'm hoping, ma'am,' he said. 'Thing is, those fifty nice guys are standing right outside that window. And I was wondering –'

'Of course they can!' cried Aunt Gardenia, drinking the remains of her cocktail. 'Ask them all in immediately!'

Barney Loot pulled up the window and blew an ear-splitting whistle.

A minute later, fifty men in blue overalls covered in black arrows clambered into the room.

Miasma made cocktails for everyone. Osbert Codseye and Barney Loot danced with Aunt Gardenia and Polly and George laughed until they almost fell out of their chairs.

Then out of the corner of his eye, George saw Rupert Cudgel's face crumple with rage. Amelia Whinge seemed to be made out of stone.

They glared around the room, saving their most poisonous look for Aunt Gardenia. Then they stood up from the table and left.

A white card lay on the floor underneath Rupert Cudgel's chair. George picked it up, whispered to Polly and the two of them crept into the front hall.

Polly looked at the card.

Rupert Cudgel & Amelia Whinge
Hotel Inspectors
Cross Us and You're Crossed Off

was written in heavy black letters.

'Oh, no!' cried Polly. 'Now we'll never save Creakie Hall!'

And before she could stop herself, she burst into tears.

CHAPTER 6

'WHAT'S WRONG?' ASKED Miasma, putting a cold white hand on Polly's shoulder.

'Don't you like the Bullfrog Band?' said Marmaduke in a hurt voice.

Polly wiped away her tears. Marmaduke and Miasma had changed again. They were dressed in the clothes they wore when Polly and George had first met them in the attic.

'It's not that,' said George, trying to keep his voice steady. 'The Bullfrog Band is brilliant. It's this.' He

showed them the card. 'It means Creakie Hall won't be a hotel after all.'

'And it will have to be sold,' cried Polly, tears pouring down her face again.

Miasma and Marmaduke read the card carefully. 'Are you telling me that those two horrible people will say nasty things about Creakie Hall?' said Miasma in a low, dangerous voice.

'And that other people will believe them and not come and stay?' said Marmaduke, slowly.

Polly and George nodded.

'And there's nothing we can do to stop them,' said George.

'We'd better tell Aunt Gardenia,' said Polly miserably.

Miasma's green eyes glittered. 'You'll do no such thing,' she said.

'We're here to help.' She looked at Marmaduke who met her eyes and nodded mysteriously.

'Leave it to us,' he said, touching the hilt of his sword.

'You mustn't hurt them!' cried Polly.

'Who said we'd *hurt* them?' said Miasma. She grinned her wolfish grin. 'We might *haunt* them, though.'

Marmaduke laughed. 'We *are* ghosts, after all.'

And before Polly and George could reply, Marmaduke and Miasma had disappeared.

Rupert Cudgel lay on his back, snoring. There was a smug, piggy look on his face and his hands twitched as if he was writing something.

A piece of paper lay on his bed. At the top, it said: *Strictly Confidential. Inspector's Report on Creakie Hall Hotel.*

Marmaduke floated down to get a closer look. The first sentence was a list of words. Words like *atrocious*, *appalling* and *abominable*.

Rupert Cudgel snorted in his sleep. His hand twitched again.

'Disgusting, deplorable, dirty,' he muttered.

Marmaduke glided over to the bed. 'Did you say Creakie Hall Hotel was *dirty*?' he whispered.

Rupert Cudgel turned over. 'Dirty, dusty, dreary,' he mumbled.

Marmaduke's eyes glowed like hot coals. He held out a white hand and passed it over Rupert Cudgel's blotchy red face.

Rupert Cudgel moaned and then he had the strangest dream. He dreamt he was in a room with other people. Other very important people. And he dreamt that the moment he spoke, his too-tight pinstripe suit burst and he stood looking like a pig in spotted underpants. Worst of all, he dreamt that everyone laughed and laughed.

And it happened again and again and again.

'Oh, no!' shouted Rupert Cudgel in his sleep.

'Oh, yes!' cried Marmaduke. Then he leaned forward. 'But you can stop it, if you want.'

'How?' shouted Rupert. 'I'll do anything, *anything*!'

Marmaduke wailed in his most ghostly voice, 'Write – a – good – report – for – Creakie – Hall – Hotel!' He was beginning to wonder if he had missed out on a whole lot of fun these past three hundred years.

Rupert Cudgel tossed and turned.

'I promise, I promise.' And his hand began to twitch again. 'Superb, splendid, first-rate,' he muttered.

'That's much better,' moaned Marmaduke. Then he disappeared in a silvery mist that floated out of the window.

Amelia Whinge was packed and ready to go. The truth was she hadn't liked the look of Creakie Hall in the first place. Not enough beige and plastic and brand new furniture.

And as for that silly woman with her sweet smile and bag of knitting. She should be chained to a rocking chair in some old people's home. Hotels should be run by businessmen.

Amelia Whinge's lips were pressed together in a tight line. Even when she was asleep, her face looked prim and prissy.

Miasma floated over to the side of the bed to get a better look at the report that was lying on the table. It was short and to the point. *Don't come. It's a dump,* was written in Amelia Whinge's neat, mean handwriting.

Miasma stared at it. The word *dump* went round and round her mind like a silver bullet in a pinball machine. It was not a word she liked at all.

Miasma's green eyes glowed like exploding stars. She held out a white hand and passed it over Amelia Whinge's nasty, pinched face.

Amelia Whinge moaned. Then she had the strangest dream. She dreamt that she wasn't a clever hotel inspector who was better than everyone else. She dreamt she was a huge muscle-bound weight-lifter whose favourite hobby was wrestling in mud.

Amelia Whinge sat bolt upright.

'Oh, no!' she shrieked.

'Oh yes,' whispered Miasma. Then she leaned forward. 'But you can stop it, if you want.'

'How?' moaned Amelia. 'I'll do anything, *anything*!'

'Write – a – good – report – for – Creakie – Hall – Hotel,' wailed Miasma. 'And – never – come – here – again!'

'I promise, I promise,' mumbled Amelia, falling back on her pillow and wiping tiny pearls of sweat from her forehead.

'That's better,' grinned Miasma. Then she lifted up the sheet and put a bullfrog into Amelia Whinge's bed.

The next morning Polly and George woke up from a deep, refreshing sleep.

'Good morning, dears,' said Aunt Gardenia. She was standing on the doorstep watching Rupert Cudgel and Amelia Whinge drag their suitcases over to their big black car. Their faces were ashen and their legs were trembling so much they could hardly walk.

Aunt Gardenia smiled.

'What lovely people,' she said. 'They told me they had such a restful time they could barely stand.' She held a white card in her hand. 'What's more, they're hotel inspectors and they have promised to write a first-rate report for Creakie Hall.'

Polly sat down on the stairs. She was so relieved that for a moment her own legs felt weak and wobbly.

'What's that big parcel on the table?' asked George.

'It's a present from Mr Loot,' replied Aunt Gardenia.

She opened the card beside it. '*Dear Miss Gardenia*,' she read.

'*Congratulations! Creakie Hall Hotel is the greatest. Take my word for it, people will come from miles away just to hear the Bullfrog Band.*

Your friend,

Barney Loot.

P.S. Here's a little something from us all.'

'What is it?' asked Polly.

'A box of chocolates, I expect,' said Aunt Gardenia. She handed the parcel to George.

'It's very heavy for a box of chocolates,' said George.

He pulled away the paper.

'Goodness me,' said Aunt Gardenia.

'What a pretty brick.'

'It's not a brick,' said Osbert Codseye from the dining-room door. 'It's a gold bar.'

'A gold bar!' cried Aunt Gardenia. For the first time ever Aunt Gardenia looked pink and flustered. 'How extraordinary!'

'It's not extraordinary,' cried Polly. 'It's wonderful! Now Creakie Hall won't fall down.'

Aunt Gardenia thought of all those letters on her desk.

'I can write to the builder, the plumber, the electrician –'

'And we can buy a brand new lawn mower!' shouted George.

Osbert Codseye could barely believe his ears! A brand new lawn mower! It was more than he could have ever hoped for! It was his wildest dream!

Thud! Osbert Codseye sank to the floor. Polly looked up at the two portraits hanging in the front hall.

'Where are Marmaduke and Miasma? she asked.

'They've gone, too,' said Aunt Gardenia. She shrugged. 'Something about a card game.'

Polly looked at George.

'Did they say they'd come back?' asked George.

Aunt Gardenia nodded.

'Any time we needed them.' She picked up her enormous bag of knitting. 'Come along, Osbert,' she said, prodding him with her foot. 'You and I have work to do.'

Polly and George stood alone in the front hall staring at the portraits of Miasma and Marmaduke Bogey-Mandeville. There was something different about them.

Instead of a sword hilt, Marmaduke's hand was resting on the end of a meat cleaver. And Miasma had a feather duster tucked under her arm.

About the Author

Karen Wallace was born in Canada and spent her childhood messing about on the river in the backwoods of Quebec. Now she lives in Herefordshire with her husband, the author Sam Llewellyn.

For more information about *The Ghosts of Creakie Hall* series and other Catnip books visit

www.catnippublishing.co.uk